BIRD DOGS CAN'T FLY

written and illustrated by

MARY JANE AUCH

Holiday House/New York

Library of Congress Cataloging-in-Publication Data
Auch, Mary Jane.
    Bird dogs can't fly / written and illustrated by Mary Jane Auch.—1st ed.
        p.   cm.
    Summary: A bird dog befriends an injured wild goose, and on foot they head south for the winter.
    ISBN 0-8234-1050-1
    [1. Dogs—Fiction.   2. Geese—Fiction.   3. Friendship—Fiction.]   I. Title.
    PZ7.A898Bi   1993   93-2746   CIP   AC
    [E]—dc20

For Nancy Jordan

It was duck season, and Blue had to go hunting with his owner. He dreaded it. He hated picking up the dead ducks in his mouth and carrying them back to the boat. One day, Blue's owner took aim at a line of wild geese. BANG! A goose dropped into the marsh.

"Fetch, Blue," said the hunter. Blue had never retrieved a goose before. He had always admired the lovely long-necked birds flying overhead in their V-shaped lines. Blue dragged his feet as he followed his keen nose to the goose.

"Stand back, dog," she hissed.

"I won't hurt you," said Blue. "Are you all right?"

"My wing is injured. I can't fly."

"Hurry up, you lazy bird dog!" Blue's owner shouted.

"I have to go," said Blue, "but I'll come back later."

That night, Blue's owner sent him to the barn without any supper. "Stupid dog. You didn't bring back the one bird I shot today—a goose at that."

When the last light went out in the house, Blue slipped away to the marsh. He found Goose right where he had left her. "Do you feel better?"

"I'm cold and lonely. I haven't seen any geese all day. They've gone on without me."

"I'll stay with you," said Blue. He curled up on the cold marsh grass and talked softly to Goose until she fell asleep.

The next day Blue took her an ear of corn. He carried treats to Goose every day that week, but she only got sadder and sadder.

"I have to get south," Goose said. "All the other geese are there already."

"What's South?" Blue asked.

"It's beautiful—warm breezes, sparkling water, and lots to eat."

"Is South far away?"

"I don't think so. It doesn't take long to fly there."

"I'll have to go hunting again tomorrow," said Blue. "I can't stand it anymore. I'll help you walk to South instead."

"Are you sure?" asked Goose.

"Yes. I've wanted to run away for a long time."

But South was farther away than either Blue or Goose had imagined. They walked over a hill, under a bridge, and along the edge of a forest. When Goose's feet got sore, Blue carried her. When Blue got cold, Goose kept him warm with her downy feathers.

They saw fields, farms, and cities. They saw everything but what they were looking for.

"Where *is* South?" asked Blue. "I think we're lost."

"We must be close." Goose flapped her wings. "I think I can fly again. I'll go and take a look from the air."

Blue watched Goose circle the town. "Did you see South?" he asked when she returned.

"There's nothing but snow as far as I can see," Goose said. "Finding South was always so easy. What happened?"

"You're used to flying instead of walking," said Blue.

"That's right!" said Goose. "Everything looks different from the ground. But now I can fly again."

"You're going to leave me?" Blue's heart did a little flip-flop.

"Of course not. We'll fly south together."

"But I can't fly."

"The hunter called you a *bird* dog," said Goose. "Don't you ever use your ears to fly?"

"Nobody ever told me about flying."

"It's a cinch. Just flap your ears hard."

"I'm flapping," said Blue. "Nothing's happening."

"Never mind," said Goose. "There's no time for practice. That balloon will take you up in the air. Jump in the basket."

"Is it safe?" asked Blue.

"Just hold still while I untie this knot. There, you're taking off! We'll fly south with that flock of birds overhead."

"Can't we just go by ourselves?" asked Blue.

"Don't be silly. Migration is a group thing."

"Isn't flying wonderful?" exclaimed Goose. "I'm beginning to feel like my old self again."

"I . . . I've never been this far from the ground," said Blue, but Goose was too busy to hear him.

"Straighten up these lines," she honked at the other birds. "What is this, your first trip south? Who's in charge?"

"Don't get them mad," Blue whispered. "Those beaks look sharp."

"Well, somebody has to whip them into shape. Make a *V*, not a *Q*! Don't you know your alphabet?" yelled Goose.

Suddenly the birds swooped in and pecked holes in Blue's balloon. Luckily, he landed in a snowdrift.

"I told you they were getting mad," said Blue. "Let's stop at this farm to sleep. We can figure out what to do in the morning."

"OK," said Goose. "All that flying has made me tired."

That night, the two friends huddled together to keep warm. Blue must have fallen asleep, because he never heard the footsteps.

"Look at that poor dog," said a woman's voice. "He's shivering."

"Look at that plump goose," said the man.

"Maybe these people will give us something to eat," whispered Blue.

"I'm getting out of here!" honked Goose. "People scare me." With a roar of wing feathers, she took off.

"Please don't leave me!" Blue cried, but Goose was already high in the air.

The woman reached down and petted Blue. "Come on, boy. You need a good meal and a warm bed."

Blue looked back and saw Goose silhouetted against the full moon. Sadly, he followed the woman into the house.

Blue felt better after eating, but he was worried about Goose. Could she fly south all by herself? What if she got lost in a winter storm? Worse yet, what if another hunter shot her?

Later that night, Blue heard a familiar honking. He barked at the door and was let outside. "Goose! I thought I'd never see you again."

"I came back to check on you. I don't trust humans."

"These people are different," Blue told her. "They'll take care of us. We don't need to find South."

"*I* do. I'm a wild goose. I can't help it."

"But Christmas is coming any day now," said Blue. "People give presents to their pets, and they'll have a big dinner with lots of leftovers for us. Can't we at least stay until after Christmas dinner?"

"If it means that much to you," said Goose, "I'll hide in the barn for a few days. No longer, though."

The next night Blue overheard the couple talking about Christmas dinner. "I've made the sweet potato pie, cranberry sauce, and plum pudding," said the woman. "Tonight I'll mix the chestnut dressing."

Blue's mouth watered. There would be some fine leftovers from a feast like that.

The man picked up an ax from the wood box. "I'll go kill that goose in the barn. She should go into the oven first thing in the morning."

Kill Goose? Blue pushed ahead of the man. "Goose, you're in danger!" he howled. But the barn door was shut tight. Could Goose even hear him?

"Stop that racket," the man yelled. "You'll scare off our Christmas dinner." When he opened the barn door, Goose thundered past him. "Stupid dog! Now look what you've done!"

Blue ran into the darkness. He could hear the man shouting behind him. Then he heard Goose, high in the night sky. "Follow me!" she called. "I'm heading south. I can feel it."

Blue ran after Goose for hours, but it was hard to keep up with her. Just before dawn he called out, "I can't go on!" But Goose was too far away to hear. Blue collapsed into an exhausted sleep.

The next morning something poked Blue's ear.

"Tah-dah!" said Goose. "I came back to wake you up." She nudged him to his feet.

"Where are we?" asked Blue.

"This is South," said Goose. "We were much closer than I thought. Come on, let's go swimming."

She led him to the edge of the sparkling water. They splashed and swam. Then Blue let his ears dry in the warm breeze. Later, when he got hungry, people on the beach shared their picnic lunches with him.

South turned out to be everything Goose had promised. Blue's favorite part of every day was going for walks with Goose. She made him see the world in a whole new way. Blue had never known a better friend.

The weeks passed quickly until one day, Goose seemed restless. "It's spring," she said. "Time to fly north for the summer."

"But I love South," said Blue. "I don't want to leave."

"I *have* to go. Geese migrate every spring."

"Can't you stay?" begged Blue. "Please?"

"I'll try," said Goose.

In the next few days, line after line of geese took off, filling the air with their wild chorus. Goose stayed by Blue's side until nature's pull was too strong for her. "I have to go with them," she said finally. "I'm sorry."

"It's all right," said Blue, but it wasn't all right at all. He watched as his best friend spread her wings and went to join the others in their perfect *V.* He kept watching as they became tiny specks against the sky, then disappeared beyond the horizon.

Blue went for a swim, but the water didn't sparkle as much as before. The breeze didn't feel as warm, and he had no appetite for picnic lunches. He went for a walk, but nothing interested him.

Blue put his head down on his paws and looked north, toward the place where Goose had gone. He watched and waited for a long time.

Then Blue noticed a small speck on the horizon. As it came closer, the speck turned into a bird—a long-necked bird. Could it be? It was!

Blue ran to meet Goose. "You came back!" he cried. "But are you going to stay? All the other geese have gone."

"I don't need them anymore," Goose said. "You're my best friend in the whole world. . . . And best friends belong together!"